PIGGIES in PAJAMAS

MICHELLE MEADOWS   ILLUSTRATED BY ARD HOYT

Simon & Schuster Books for Young Readers   New York London Toronto Sydney New Delhi

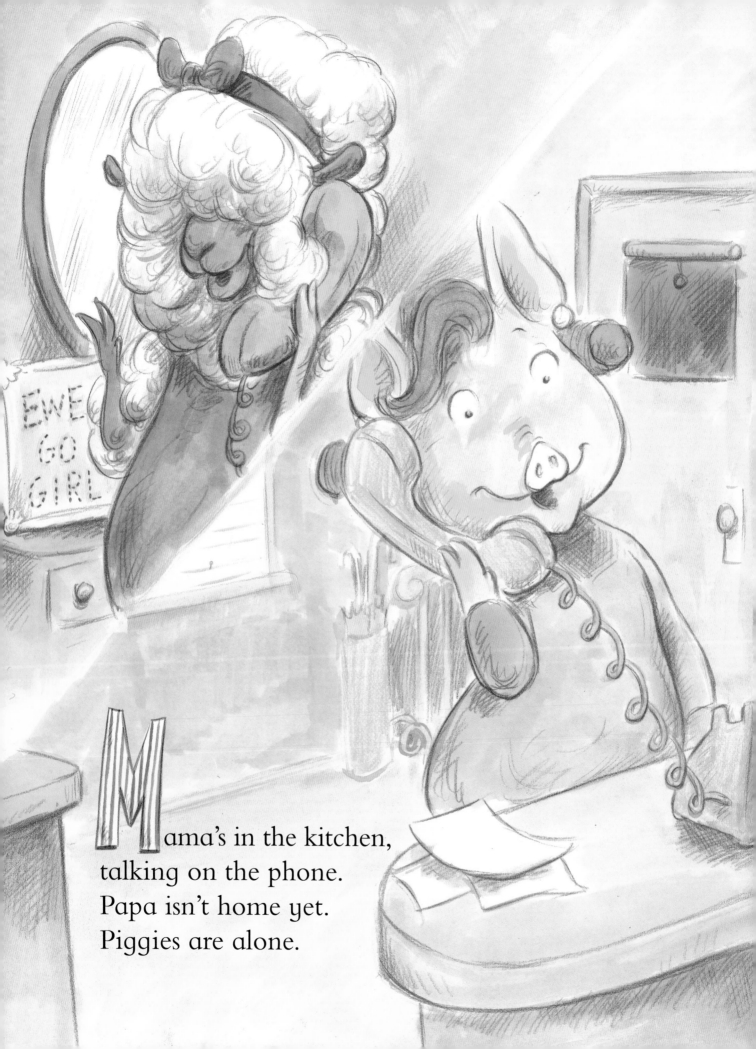

Mama's in the kitchen,
talking on the phone.
Papa isn't home yet.
Piggies are alone.

Piggies in pajamas,
jumping in the air,
tossing up the pillows,
popcorn in their hair.

Climbing up the mountain,
lined up in a row,
diving in the ocean,
piggies holler, "Go!"

THUMP, THUMP.
OINK, OINK—

All the piggies fall.

STOMP, STOMP,
STOMP,
STOMP—

"Mama's in the hall!"

Hurry to the tunnel.
Everybody, hide.
Underneath the covers,
snuggle deep inside.

CRICK, CREAK goes the door.
"Is Mama really here?"
"She's busy on the phone—
I think the coast is clear!"

Piggies in pajamas,
scoot across the floor.
Going for a train ride,
speeding past the door.

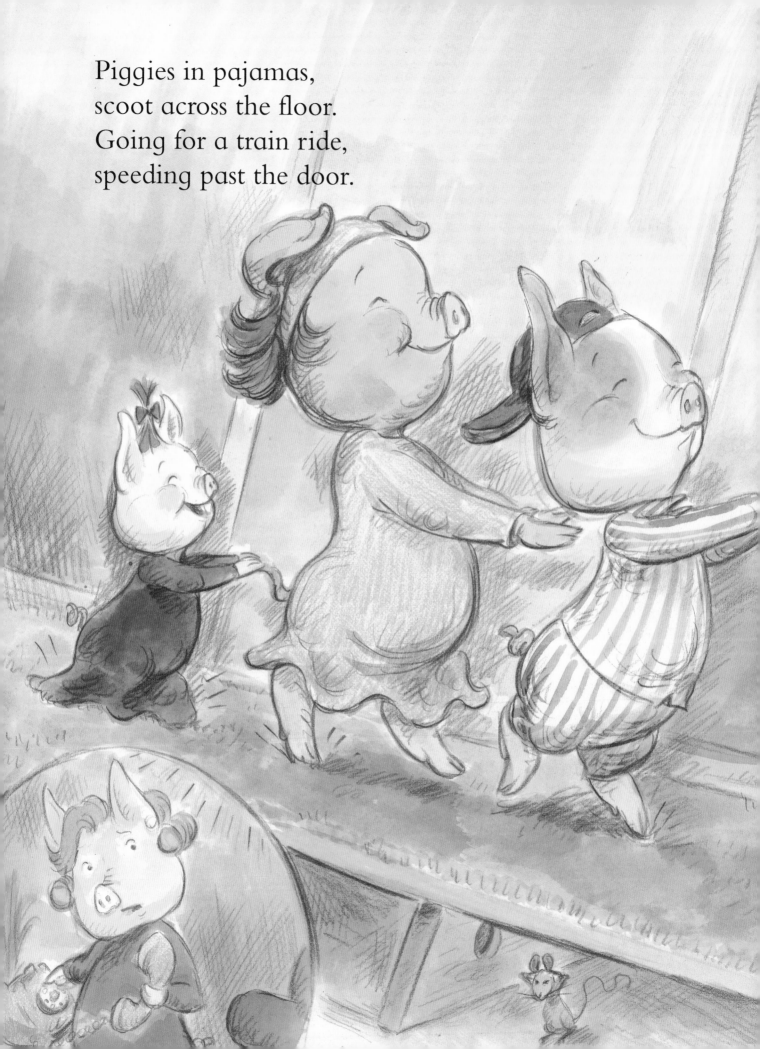

TOOT, TOOT.
OINK, OINK—
Rolling down the track.

STOMP,
STOMP,
STOMP,
STOMP—

"Mama's coming back!"

Hurry to the tunnel.
Everybody, hide.
Underneath the covers,
snuggle deep inside.

CRICK, CREAK goes the floor.
"She's sitting down to chat.
She's talking on the phone again—
I think it's Mrs. Cat."

Piggies in pajamas,
whirl around the room.
Cartwheels and somersaults—

BOOM, BOOM,
BOOM!

BOOM, BOOM, OINK, OINK—

Piggies love to play.

STOMP, STOMP, STOMP, STOMP—

"Mama's on the way!"

Hurry to the tunnel.
Everybody, hide.
Underneath the covers,
snuggle deep inside.

CRICK, CREAK goes the door.
"Is Mama coming back?"
"She's heading to the kitchen,
looking for a snack."

Piggies in pajamas,
digging through the chest:
race cars, tambourines,
a polka-dotted vest!

"Who's at the window?"
Piggies drop their toys.

SCRITCH, SCRATCH, TAP, TAP—
"What's that noise?!"

Just a little tree branch
that gives the pigs a scare.
But they think it's a wolf
or a fox or a bear!

Piggies in pajamas,
sneaking down the hall.
Crawling with their blankets.
Baby drags a doll.

Mama's in the bathroom,
washing up her face.

Piggies in pajamas,
find a cozy place.

TICKLE, TICKLE.
OINK, OINK—

They giggle for a while.

SNUGGLE,
SNUGGLE.
GOOD NIGHT—
Piggies in a pile.

Mama sees their pink ears.
Tails are sticking out.

Mama climbs into bed and
kisses every snout.
"Good night, piggies!"

For Max and Wilhelmina,
the cutest piggies in New York
—M. M.

For the Parmelee family
—A. H.

SIMON & SCHUSTER BOOKS FOR YOUNG READERS
An imprint of Simon & Schuster Children's Publishing Division · 1230 Avenue of the Americas, New York, New York 10020
Text copyright © 2013 by Michelle Meadows · Illustrations copyright © 2013 by Ard Hoyt
SIMON & SCHUSTER BOOKS FOR YOUNG READERS is a trademark of Simon & Schuster, Inc.
For information about special discounts for bulk purchases, please contact Simon & Schuster Special Sales at 1–866–506–1949 or
business@simonandschuster.com. · The Simon & Schuster Speakers Bureau can bring authors to your live event. For more information
or to book an event, contact the Simon & Schuster Speakers Bureau at 1–866–248–3049 or visit our website at www.simonspeakers.com.
Book design by Chloë Foglia based on a design by Jessica Handelman · The text for this book is set in Bembo Infant.
The illustrations for this book are rendered in pen and ink with watercolor on Arches paper. · Manufactured in China · 1212 SCP
2 4 6 8 10 9 7 5 3 1
Library of Congress Cataloging-in-Publication Data
Meadows, Michelle.
Piggies in pajamas / Michelle Meadows ; illustrated by Ard Hoyt.—1st ed.
p. cm.
Summary: Piggies try to stay up as long as they can as their mother gets ready for bed.
ISBN 978-1-4169-4982-4 (hardcover)
ISBN 978-1-4424-6865-8 (eBook)
[1. Stories in rhyme. 2. Pigs—Fiction. 3. Bedtime—Fiction.] I. Hoyt, Ard, ill. II. Title.
PZ8.3.M4625Pg 2012
[E]—dc22
2010024472

MAR – – 2013